RITA PHILLIPS MITCHELL started writing in 1988, when she joined the Islington Writers' Group. She was a teacher for over twenty years, and headteacher of a primary school for twelve of those years. The author was born and educated in Belize, although she moved to England to study for her Open University degree and teacher training. She has travelled widely, often returning to her family home in Belize. Rita Phillips Mitchell now works part-time, teaching English as a second language, and giving basic counselling. She is married, with one grown-up son, and lives in Essex. *Hue Boy* is her first published story.

CAROLINE BINCH is a widely admired artist whose first full-colour picture book, *Billy the Great*, was written by Rosa Guy and published by Gollancz to great acclaim. She has previously provided the humorous, eye-catching black and white illustrations for a popular series of Dick Cate's children's novels, and is well-known for her stunning jacket illustrations for adult and children's novels. Caroline Binch lives in Cornwall.

Hue Boy won the Smarties Book Prize (0-5 Category) and was Highly Commended for the Kate Greenaway Medal in 1993.

For Leann and Brian
RPM

For Enid and for Wilf
CB

PUFFIN BOOKS

Published by the Penguin Group
Penguin Books Ltd, 27 Wrights Lane, London W8 5TZ, England
Penguin Books USA Inc., 375 Hudson Street, New York, New York 10014, USA
Penguin Books Australia Ltd, Ringwood, Victoria, Australia
Penguin Books Canada Ltd, 10 Alcorn Avenue, Toronto, Ontario, Canada M4V 3B2
Penguin Books (NZ) Ltd, 182–190 Wairau Road, Auckland 10, New Zealand

Penguin Books Ltd, Registered Offices: Harmondsworth, Middlesex, England

First published by Victor Gollancz Ltd 1992
Published in Victor Gollancz Children's Paperbacks 1994
This edition published in Puffin Books 1997
10 9 8 7 6 5 4 3 2

Text copyright © Rita Phillips Mitchell, 1992
Illustrations copyright © Caroline Binch, 1992
All rights reserved

The moral right of the author and illustrator has been asserted

Made and printed in Italy by Printers srl – Trento

British Library Cataloguing in Publication Data
A CIP catalogue record for this book is available from the British Library

ISBN 0–140–56354–7

RITA PHILLIPS MITCHELL

HUE
BOY

illustrated by
Caroline Binch

PUFFIN BOOKS

Little Hue Boy was big news in his village. He was so small that all his friends towered over him.

Every morning Hue Boy's mother measured him.
   "Come, I must measure you before you go to school," she said. "Stand straight against the wall."
   It did not matter how straight Hue Boy stood, he remained the same size — very small. He didn't grow at all, at all.
   "Oh lawd!" cried Hue Boy's mother. "I wish your father was home. He would know what to do about this."
   But Hue Boy knew his father was working on a ship, far away.

Then one day Mum said, "Hue Boy, if you want to grow tall you must eat fresh vegetables and fruit every day."

"Like pumpkins?" said Hue Boy. "I like pumpkin soup."

"Pumpkins are good. But what about spinach, Hue Boy?"

"Yuck!" Hue Boy said. "I don't like spinach! I'd rather have fruit, like mangoes and melons."

"And pineapples and sapodillas, I suppose?" said Mum.

"Mm, yum, yum," said Hue Boy.

"How about sweet-sops, cashews and craboos?" his mother asked.

"Yes," said Hue Boy, "Delicious! And don't forget guavas or tamarinds, either."

"I won't, Hue Boy," said Mum.

Hue Boy was soon eating everything his mother gave him. The pumpkin soup was delicious, but he enjoyed eating fruit best.

Still, Hue Boy didn't grow one little bit. He didn't grow at all, at all.

On Hue Boy's birthday, his grandmother gave him
a special present.

"I've made you new clothes," she said. "You'll soon
grow into them."

Hue Boy tried on the clothes. They felt a little loose.

"Lawdy! You look taller already," said Gran.

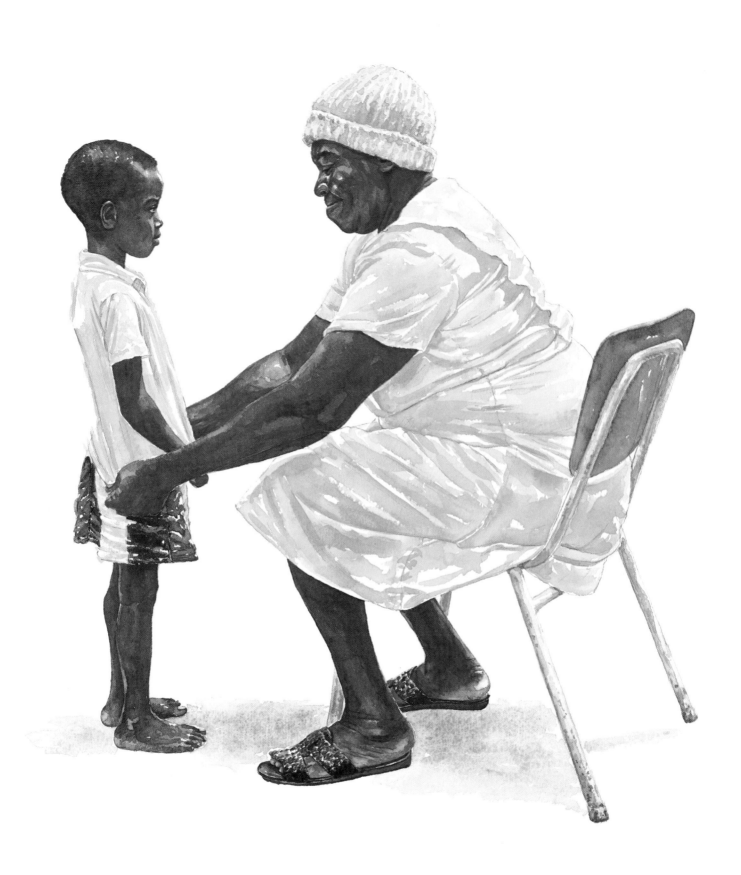

Then one morning, their
neighbour Carlos said,
"I know, Hue Boy.
Some stretching exercises
will do the trick. Ten minutes
a day. That's all you need to do."

And so Hue Boy began
to do all sorts of exercises.
He stretched as much
as he could.

Still, Hue Boy didn't grow
one little bit. He didn't grow
at all, at all.

At school his classmates chanted:
    "Heels, heels, high heeled shoes,
        Needed for the smallest boy in the school."
Hue Boy looked down.

But Miss Harper, the teacher, said, "Stuff and nonsense! Walk tall, Hue Boy. Hold your head up. That's all you need to do!"

Still Hue Boy didn't grow one little bit.
He didn't grow at all, at all.

Hue Boy's mother was worried. "Come, we must look for some help in the village," she said.

First they went to see the wisest man in the village. "Please, can you help Hue Boy to grow like other children?" said Mum.
   The wise man of the village looked at Hue Boy from head to toe. Then from toe to head. "Well, Hue Boy," he said. "Where help is not needed, no help can be given."

Next they visited Doctor Gamas. He examined Hue Boy thoroughly.

Then he said, "There is absolutely nothing wrong with you, Hue Boy. Some people are short and perfectly healthy, you know."

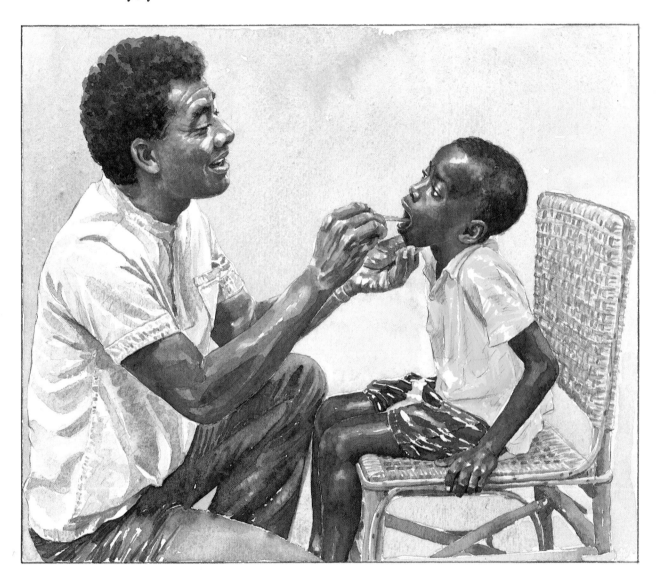

"Lawdy," cried Mum. "This problem seems to be bigger than this village!"

She thought carefully. "We ought to try Miss Frangipani, the Healer," she said. "Maybe she can help."

Hue Boy sighed. "I hope so."

"Miss Frangipani," said Mum.
"Please! Can you do something
for Hue Boy to make him grow?"
  "No problem," said Miss Frangipani.
"I alone hold the secret to growing!"

Miss Frangipani placed
a hand on Hue Boy's head
and said:

  "Ooooo! Ooooo!
  Grow-o, Grow-o.
  A touch of the hand;
  A wish of the mind,
  Comes the cure from far away.
  Ooooo! Ooooo!
  Grow-o, Grow-o.
  As you're meant to do."

Then Miss Frangipani gave
Hue Boy a bundle of herbs.
  "You must have your bath
with these," she told him.
"Mind you do it every night."

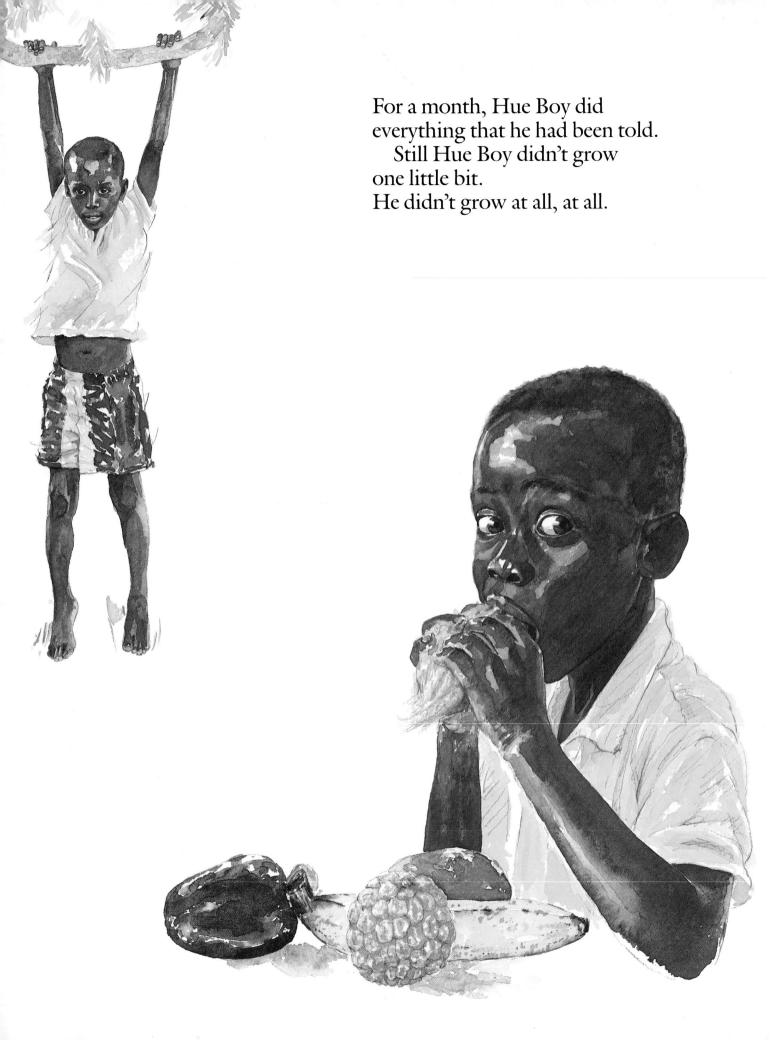

For a month, Hue Boy did
everything that he had been told.
    Still Hue Boy didn't grow
one little bit.
He didn't grow at all, at all.

Sometimes Hue Boy liked to go
to the harbour. There he watched
the ships come and go and he could
forget about his size.
   One day a beautiful big ship came in.
   Man, that looks good! thought Hue Boy.
It's the biggest ship I ever saw!

Then Hue Boy saw a very tall man among
the passengers. The tall man walked
straight towards him.
　"Hello, Hue Boy," he said.
　"Dad!" said Hue Boy.

His father took Hue Boy's hand
and they walked away from
the harbour and into the village.

They walked past Miss Frangipani.
    They walked past Doctor Gamas
and the wisest man in the village.
    They walked past Miss Harper and Carlos.
    And they walked past Hue Boy's
friends from school.
    Then they met Gran and Mum.

And Hue Boy walked tall, with his head held high.
    He was the happiest boy in the village.

And then something happened to Hue Boy. He began to grow.
At first he grew just a little bit. Then he grew a little more.
Until the time came when his size didn't worry him anymore.

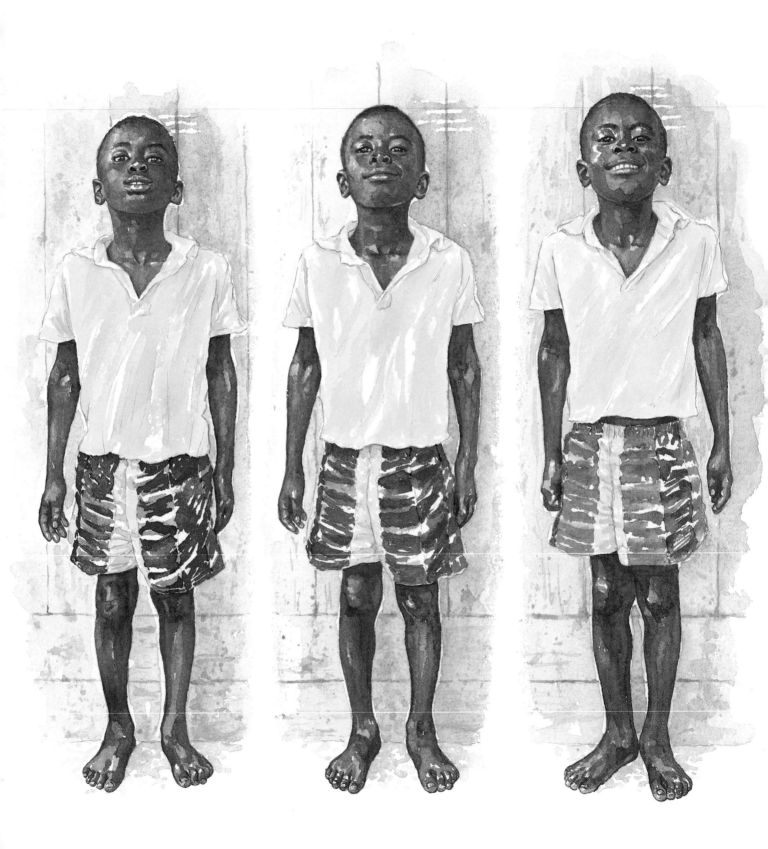